MAGGIE'S AMERIKAY

BARBARA TIMBERLAKE RUSSELL
Pictures by JIM BURKE

MELANIE KROUPA BOOKS
Farrar, Straus and Giroux ☆ New York

When we set sail for America,
Da played a jig on his tin whistle
so that none of us would cry for leaving.
"Maggie McCrary," he told me,
"in Amerikay, we will start anew."

New Orleans, 1898

From our room in New Orleans, Mam calls, "No dawdling after lessons, Maggie. Bessie needs watching if I'm to finish sewing." Can't make a dollar to buy land in America reading and learning sums, that's what her weary eyes tell me. But Da says so long as he draws breath, his daughters will be educated. Book learning and feverish hard work—is this why we have left our home and family?

But I hold my tongue when the neighbor girls who stay home to roll cigars call out "Miss High and Mighty" as I pass them with my books on my way to school. I stamp my foot and they scatter, laughing. Who wants this Amerikay, I think as I march ahead. At least in Ireland we had friends to stand beside us.

On Esplanade, I run to catch up with Da's pushcart. He sings:

Your every want, your every need!
Bottles, balms, and a baby's buggy!

A woman waves us over.

"How may I help, madam?" Da asks.

"Boot laces, sir." The woman's eyes soften as she smiles, but I don't smile back. I've been told to stay away from such Negroes. "They take our work," our neighbors say.

While the woman sorts through the laces, her children's eyes roam about the shelves of Da's cart, lined with tins and old clothes and boxes of trinkets. But I know exactly where her boy's gaze will fall. As usual, he's admiring the dented cornet Da traded for an old coat last winter.

"Your Nathan has the makings of a musician, madam," Da says as he takes a penny for the laces.

"A ragtime musician," Nathan says.

I myself have never heard of such.

"Music won't fill his stomach," his mother says. "We have stalls to tend at market." Then I hear her tell Nathan, "Don't let me catch you fooling with Irish, boy. They're trouble, you hear?"

Before she hurries him away, Nathan's eyes meet mine.

"Poor lad," Da says. "He yearns for that cornet, as I once yearned for my own tin whistle."

I squeeze his hand. "Da, that cornet could bring a full dollar."

Hadn't Mrs. O'Reilly said only yesterday, "Your father is too softhearted, giving away this and that for naught. He'll never buy land in America."

"A dollar canna buy everything, Maggie," Da says. "Mercy, let's deliver you to school before they have my whiskers."

On the way, we sing the peddler song.

That afternoon, as we load our pushcart at the market, I spot Nathan selling fish and think of the cornet. "You should hear the lad honking that old horn," Da says, as if he's read my mind.

"Da!" I scold. "You'll put ideas in his head, letting him play."

Da smiles. "Every note reveals his heart, Maggie. The boy is a musician."

My breath catches as I spot the empty place on the pushcart shelf. "Where is the cornet, Da?" I ask.

Da just closes his eyes and sings loudly:

Your every want, your every need!
Pins, pots, petticoats!

Early the next morning, milk won't keep Bessie quiet. She cries and cries. "Something's wrong," I tell Mam.

By eight, the neighbor woman comes. "It's yellow fever," she says.

She brews a strong black pepper tea. Mam will be too busy looking after Bessie to sew now.

Da says, "Maggie, get along to school. You'd best stay with Mrs. O'Reilly till Bessie's well." He looks as dismal as I have ever seen him. I know he is thinking of the babies lost to fever on our voyage from Ireland. Without Mam's sewing wages, I wonder, too: how will we keep our room, much less buy land in Amerikay?

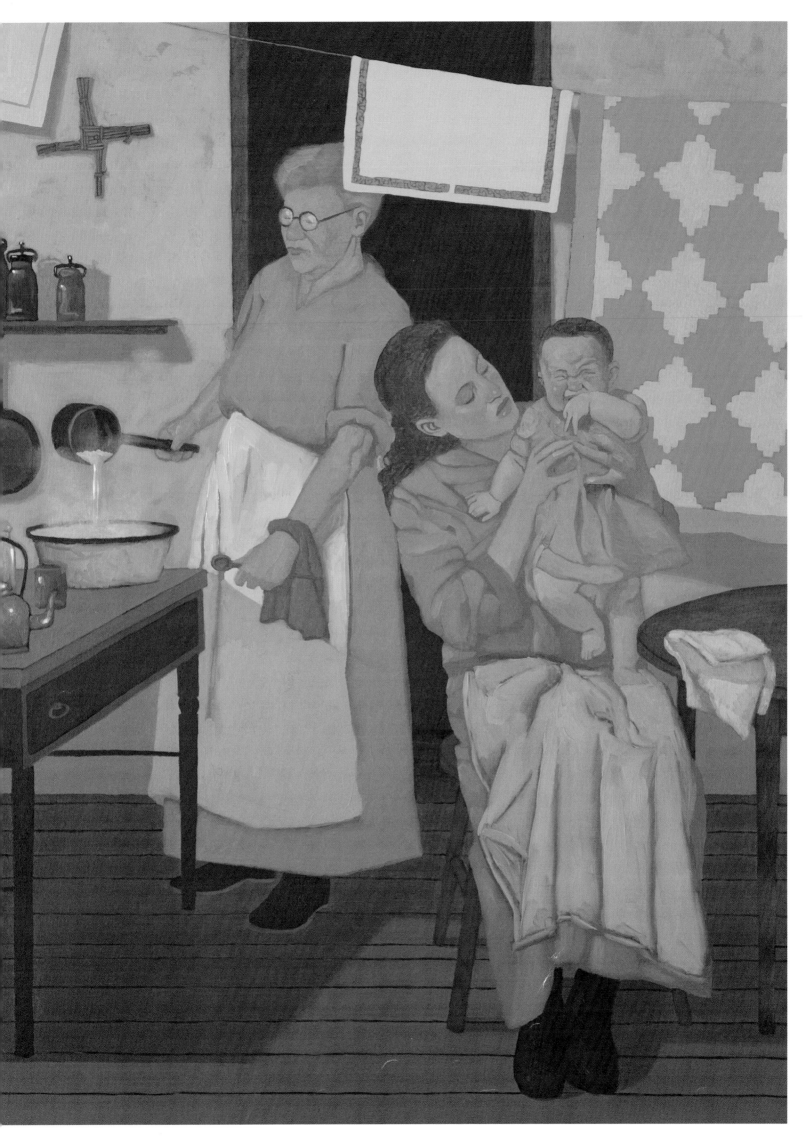

I run out the door and down to Flanagan's Pub. I can't waste time book learning in school when my family needs me.

"Would you be wanting a girl to crack walnuts?" I ask Mrs. Flanagan.

" 'Tis the Campanello sisters' job," she says.

At the candy shop, I tell the mistress, "I can learn to make pralines."

The woman shakes her head. "Family only, chère."

At the docks, Mr. Burnley says I could sew buttons on coats or make flowers or spin cotton at Shubert's factory by the wharf, but his own boss vows he'll not hire a child under twelve to crack oysters. Not enough strength for the long days, he claims. Mrs. Burnley runs her fingers over my palms. "Soft," she says. "Best stick to your schooling."

As I set out to ask Mr. Shubert for a job, I'm thinking of Da's words: "I've not crossed an ocean for my girls to work in factories."

Then a voice calls, "Maggie McCrary, where've you been, child?" It is Mrs. O'Reilly, our neighbor. "Stop your fretting," she says. "You can work with us after school till your sister is well." That very day, I begin rolling cigars. At night, I lie awake wondering how fifty cents a week will ever make up Mam's wages.

When I fall asleep at school, the teacher sends me to the corner. It's torture trying to write and read when my fingertips are split from wrapping tobacco leaves and my eyes ache from working in the O'Reillys' dim light.

The next day, Nathan catches up to me on the sidewalk. "What's wrong?" he asks when he sees my face.

Anger boils to my fingertips when I spot the dented cornet. "I've no time for talk. I must find a way to make a decent wage," I say, hoping Nathan feels wicked about taking Da's cornet.

"I know somebody looking to hire." Nathan shrugs. "But you ain't right for the job."

"Why not?" I ask, recalling what Nathan's mam said about us Irish.

"It's in Storyville," Nathan says.

I have heard tales about Storyville, about the wildness that goes on there.

But with Bessie sick, Mam unable to sew, and me with nothing but soft hands and fifty cents a week, what else can I do?

"I'll do it," I tell him.

Nathan leads me down narrow streets. I hear the clop of horses'
hooves and shouts of laughter behind closed doors. Above all this is the
plinking of a piano, and the voice of someone wailing a mournful tune.

"Hurry," Nathan says. "I'm late to market." He motions me through
back streets and up some crumbling steps into a small room.

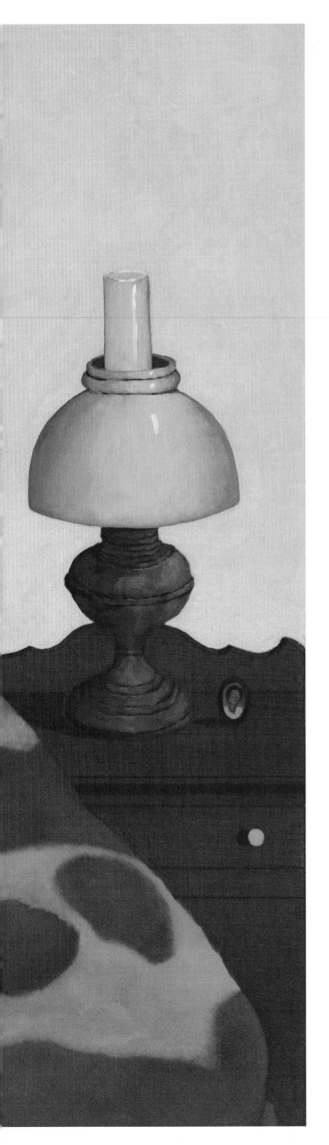

Inside, an old man is propped up in bed.

"Daddy Clements, this here girl is come to write for you."

I hold my books to my chest without breathing. Mam would skin me if she caught me here, as Da would if he found me missing school.

"Irish?" The old man scowls. "There are folks on Rampart can write, Nate. Why her?"

"I owe." Nathan holds up the cornet. "Her Daddy gave me this."

The old man looks me over. "I made my money gambling, Irish. Now what do you say?"

Words can't scare the likes of me. "I work quick and my print is plain," I tell him.

Daddy Clements nods to paper and pen. "We shall see about that."

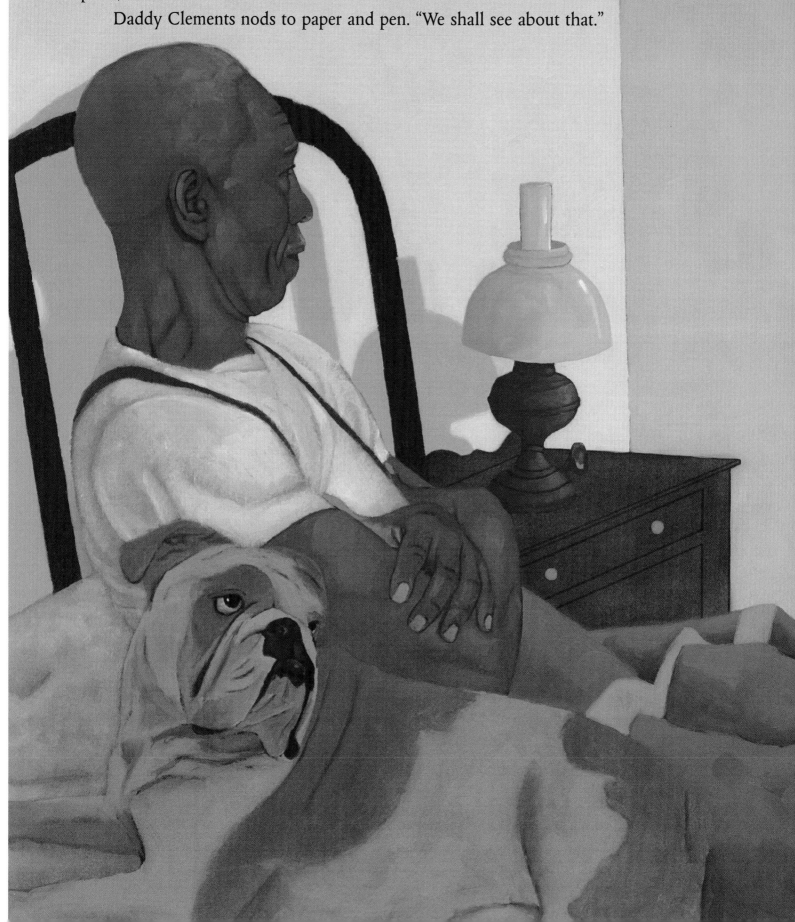

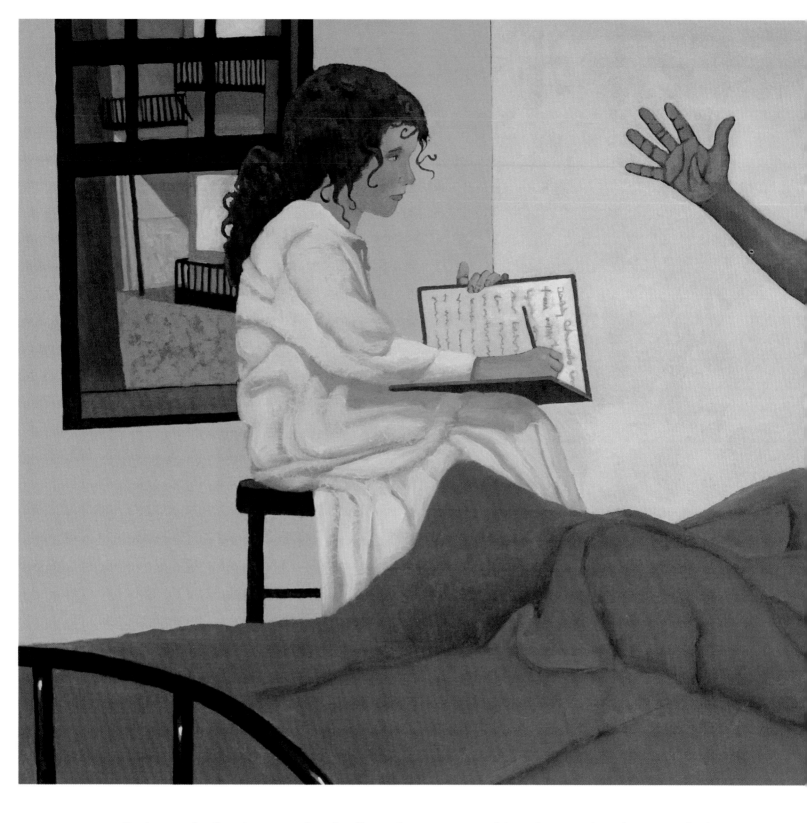

So instead of going to school, all week I write Daddy Clements's tales. Mostly he talks of how he was forced to come from Africa to America, and about his soldier years in the Civil War.

Sometimes his face stiffens like the carving on a ship's bow. "Unlike your people, mine fought to be free, Irish. We have suffered mightily to live in this country."

"We Irish fought, too." Heat rises to my face. I tell him about the battles waged in Ireland against English landowners, and about our voyage here. I tell how Da says he brought us to Amerikay to start anew.

Daddy Clements stares, then nods, as though he is recalling something. Outside, the music from the sporting houses joins the thunder of drums from the square.

"Came from Africa, those drums," he says. "Old seeds for new songs."

"Like Da's tin whistle," I tell him.

Daddy Clements leans in. "Look here, Irish, not all folks who come here to start fresh make it."

My face burns again. "But I will."

Daddy Clements laughs. "With that stubborn streak, gal, I believe you might."

As I turn to go, I wonder how I will back up my bold words.

At week's end, I tell Daddy Clements that his tales are better than most I have read in school. And to think that one day his grandchildren will read his tellings in my own hand!

At last he says, "It is fully writ, how far we have come." He pushes two dollars into my hands, more money than I have ever held. "For your start. We must stick together, Irish."

"Thank you, Daddy Clements," I tell him. But he only closes his eyes as though he is weary.

I leave soon after. As I pass through Storyville, a tune floats from inside a building, but the notes stop and start, and sometimes break apart. When I peek inside a doorway, I can't believe what I see.

A group of musicians are letting Nathan play along. I do as Da says then, listen to hear his heart. His music seems to say: *Free! Free! I choose who I will be!*

My hands begin to clap, and my feet stamp in time. Then, within me, my own song rises like a wild, free spirit. I'll work for Mam's land. I'll book learn for Da. But who I become in this land called America, that is mine. And what with my stubborn will, Daddy Clements's stories, and two dollars in my pocket, I have my start.

When the song ends, I clap loudly, then curtsy to Nathan. He tips his hat, and his eyes smile behind the dented cornet.

When I reach our street, a man with a doctor's bag is leaving our building. Not Bessie, I pray, don't let Bessie be gone.

But Bessie is in Mam's lap, taking milk while Da plays soft on his tin whistle. Mam looks up when she hears me. "She's better," she says.

I give Da my money. "I wanted to help," I say. "I wrote a man's rememberings."

"And earned such wages?" Mam asks, amazed.

Outside, over the clop of horses' hooves, I hear drums and horns. The rhythm reminds me of Nathan's ragtime. It is in the thump of Mam's boot upon the floor and in Da's tin whistle tune. It is in the squeeze of Bessie's fingers, the stamp of my foot, and in Daddy Clements's words, making a song about how far we've come and how much is learned in that wide distance.

"An Amerikay-learned modern girl," Da says. "That's our Maggie McCrary."

This time even Mam smiles. Da swings me up with one arm. Then we whirl across the room as though—in this one moment—we are all hearing the same joyful music, as though we are all singing:

Free! Free! We choose who we will be!

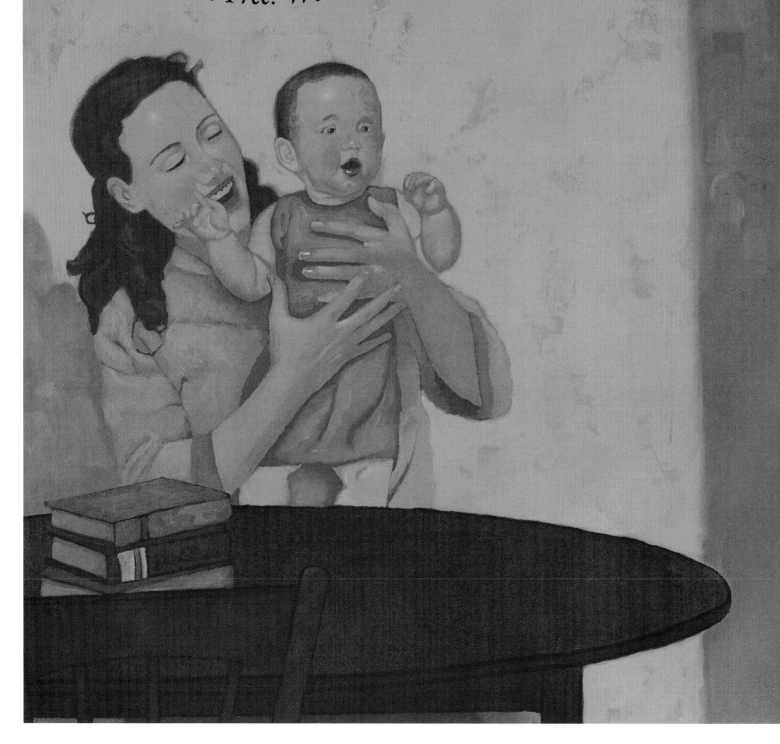

Author's Note

In the early 1800s, New Orleans was one of the most cosmopolitan and musical cities in America. French, Germans, Irish, Italians, Mexicans, Spaniards, Creoles, and many other cultural groups poured into this thriving port, hoping to find opportunity and a new home. In addition to their languages, customs, and religions, these immigrants brought their music.

New Orleans was also a center for the slave trade. Enslaved Africans had their own musical traditions, as did slaves from the West Indies and other parts of the Deep South, where work songs and spirituals were an important means of self-expression.

By the mid-1800s, New Orleans was exploding with music. On Sundays in Congo Square, slaves continued the traditional African practice of drumming and dance; marching bands played everywhere; there were even three opera companies and two symphony orchestras! With people living in crowded neighborhoods and working side by side, there seemed to be no boundaries when it came to music. What happened when all these different groups found each other was the equivalent of musical combustion.

By the end of the 1800s, music called ragtime had evolved out of this mix, and musicians were improvising and developing their own styles, creating their own unique musical "voices." Many historians today feel this new music reflected typical American values: freedom of expression and a celebration of the individual. Born in the rich mix of New Orleans' many musical traditions, this cultural watermark, like a Mississippi River breeze, lifted and restored the soul. Today we know it as jazz!

In memory of the invincible spirit of Virginia Jones. And to her sisters Anna and Holly, who carry that spirit onward. —B.T.R.

Dedicated to my Irish ancestors who found their own Amerikay: Burke, Clark, Kearns, Kelley, Martin, and McCullagh. —J.B.

Text copyright © 2006 by Barbara Timberlake Russell
Illustrations copyright © 2006 by Jim Burke
All rights reserved
Distributed in Canada by Douglas & McIntyre Ltd.
Color separations by Embassy Graphics
Printed and bound in the United States of America by Berryville Graphics
Designed by Barbara Grzeslo
First edition, 2006
1   3   5   7   9   10   8   6   4   2

www.fsgkidsbooks.com

Library of Congress Cataloging-in-Publication Data
Russell, Barbara T.
    Maggie's Amerikay / by Barbara Timberlake Russell ; pictures by Jim Burke.— 1st ed.
        p.   cm.
    Summary: In New Orleans in 1898, while her mother talks of saving to buy land and her father insists on the importance of an education, young Irish immigrant Maggie McCrary is determined to find her own way in the new place they call home.
    ISBN-13: 978-0-374-34722-2
    ISBN-10: 0-374-34722-0
    [1. Immigrants—Fiction.   2. Irish Americans—Fiction.   3. African Americans—Fiction.   4. Race Relations—Fiction.
5. Family life—Louisiana—Fiction.   6. New Orleans (La.)—History—19th century—Fiction.]   I. Burke, Jim, ill.
II. Title.

PZ7.R91536 Ma 2006
[Fic]—dc22
                                                                                                                    2005040068